TROLL

FRANCES STICKLEY
& STEFANO MARTINUZ

PUBLISHING

Below the bridge, beneath the log,
underneath the burping bog,
where townsfolk whispered, cringed and crept,
a **terrifying** monster slept.

"I think we're lost," cried Goat, and frowned.
"I'm sure the map was upside down,
for isn't this…" His voice grew weak.
"The home of whom we dare not speak?"

They say he has a heart of stone.
A hundred years he's lived alone."

"It's just a silly myth," said Hare.
"There's no such thing as—"

"It's him!" they cried. "He does exist!"
They panicked in the murky mist.
Then, scrambling through the grassy knoll,
they ran off from the dreaded...

There beneath the bridge unseen,
he found it easy to be mean.
Disguised beneath the bog and bubbles,
Troll could never get in trouble.

No one even knew his name!

So every day, he'd play his game
of hollering at everyone
and hurting feelings just for fun.

"WHO GOES THERE? HEY, THUNDER TOES!"

"I'LL SHOVE THOSE TURNIPS UP YOUR NOSE."

He sent them running, one by one.

"Excuse me, is there someone there?"

She pointed up toward her ears
and shook her head. "I cannot hear,

but please, repeat the things you said.
I'll try to read your lips instead."

Rabbit's gaze was sure and steady.
Troll was stuttering already.
"You're a… you're…" His hard heart thumped.
His tongue was tied. He was stumped.

Then as they stood there, eye to eye,
Troll felt like he might start to cry.
This wasn't right. This wasn't fun.
Anybody else would run!

She nodded at him.
"Please, go on."

But Troll found all his words were gone.

He felt embarrassed, awkward. Small.
And not much like a troll at all.

A silence settled, thick and slow,
until she said, "I think I'll go."
Just like he'd wanted all along.
So why did something feel so wrong?

A feeling stirred inside his tummy.
If he was so smart and so funny,
if he was so big and bad...

Then why did he feel small and sad?
As Rabbit left, Troll realized
he hadn't just hurt passersby.
He'd tried to troll everyone else...

... but in his hate, he'd trolled himself.
Troll was tired of this game
where no one even knew his name.

Rabbit had seemed warm and kind,
while Troll was **nasty all the time.**
But if he practiced every day,
Troll wondered... *could he smile that way?*
Then maybe... *he could have a friend?*

But first, he'd have to make amends,
to change the voice inside his head
and make friends with himself instead.

At first, he found this very tough. He simply had no ear for love.

But when he practiced every day,
he soon found kinder things to say,

like,

"HERE. I FOUND A BUTTERCUP."

And,

"WHEN YOU SMILE, YOUR EYES LIGHT UP."

As he gazed into a puddle,
Troll gave himself a gentle cuddle
and said aloud he was enough,
till all his words were made of love.

Then, as his gnarly heart unfurled...

... he found the beauty in the world.

So if you're ever near the bog,
and scramble down across the log,
just pay attention, if you dare.
You might just hear his...

.... when courage leads you to be kind.

For my sister, Anna
—F. S.

To my family and my closest friends. Don't forget to always love yourself! And to Zoë, Katie, and Frances, who believed in this book and in me as an illustrator.
—S. M.

Text © 2024 Frances Stickley
Illustrations © Stefano Martinuz
Published for North America in 2024 by Paw Prints Publishing
First published in 2024 by Magic Cat Publishing, an imprint of Lucky Cat Publishing Ltd,
Unit 2 Empress Works, 24 Grove Passage, London E2 9FQ, UK
Magic Cat Publishing, an imprint of Lucky Cat Publishing Ltd, PAKTA svetovanje d.o.o.,
Stegne 33, Ljubljana, Slovenia

No part of this publication may be reproduced, stored in a retrieval system, or transmitted, in any form, or by any means, electrical, mechanical, photocopying, recording or otherwise without the prior written permission of the publisher or a licence permitting restricted copying.

ISBN 9781223188577 HC
ISBN 9781223189413 Paperback

The illustrations were hand-drawn and coloured digitally
Set in Gelica and K26Speechbubble

Designed by Zoë Tucker

Manufactured in China

9 8 7 6 5 4 3 2 1